MW00944663

The Whiskers Gang –
Mermilo's Great Escape

Jenny M. Uzelac

Saguaro Books, LLC
SB
Arizona

Saguaro Books, LLC
16201 E. Keymar Dr.
Fountain Hills, AZ 85268
www.saguarobooks.com

ISBN: 978-1540305930
Library of Congress Cataloging Number
LCCN: 2016959242
Printed in the United States of America
First Edition

Dedication

This book is dedicated to my fourth grade class of 2010-2011 from Ishikawa Elementary School, Mesa, Arizona. You were my inspiration to continue.

Chapter 1

Tuesday morning started out just like every other morning, but it wouldn't remain that way for very long. Mermilo, a strikingly handsome purebred golden retriever, had an appointment with the dog groomer to get his coat trimmed and shampooed, and his nails clipped and manicured. He had a very important dinner date that night with the adorable poodle of his dreams who just so happened to live right across the street from his house.

As Mermilo started down the sidewalk to his favorite salon, Clausen's Clipper Clinic, his mood swelled with happiness and anticipation at how debonair he would look this evening as he would proudly trot alongside Miss Penny Purelove. His imagination began to wander. The crisp night air would ruffle his finely trimmed fur as he gazed at his beautiful companion. Her lashes would be blinking rapidly, while her eyes would be shimmering, reflecting the glow from the streetlights above. Her dainty, perfectly fashioned nails would make an elegant clicking rhythm as she pranced down the sidewalk upon her neatly groomed paws. They would both regard each other with admiring eyes. It would be the most glorious night of his dreams.

He had anxiously waited for months, trying to muster up the nerve to invite the curly-haired canine out for an evening on the town. There had been many times he started across the street only to retrace his steps because he lost every ounce of courage; his words would start to evaporate from his brain, his mouth would dry up like the sands of Death Valley, and he would start to tremble. Yes, it had been a strenuous several months until he finally decided to take the plunge and pop the question. So with all that in mind, can you blame him for wanting to look his "dog show best", as they say in the canine world?

For days and days he had anticipated how the evening would proceed, and the night was finally here. But he still had a serious problem to solve. Where would he take her? Perhaps they could get a reservation at Dagwood's Dog Biscuits Divine. No, their cuisine was too dry and overly crunchy. It would only create embarrassing crumbs upon both of their immaculately groomed coats.

Maybe they should try Baileys' Burger Bits. They had just recently been given a four star rating for catering to the canine cuisine in "Dog Diner's Directory", a weekly news guide for the trendiest canine bistros. Unfortunately, upon further thought, that also became a "no way", as their entrees were too juicy and runny and he surely didn't want to mess up his or her fresh grooming. He would really have to think this one through in order to make a huge impression on the little curly-haired poodle.

As he sauntered down Hazelnut Street towards Clausen's Clipper Clinic, his mind was heavily preoccupied in another world, totally oblivious to his surroundings.

All of a sudden, out of nowhere, everything went pitch black and his hearing became extremely muffled. His head was completely enveloped with some strange mesh-type dark colored material, pressing down heavily on his neck and restraining him so he couldn't move his head or body. He couldn't see a thing. What in the world was happening?

He struggled to breathe through his nose and mouth, his thoughts scrambling for answers as to what his next step should be. Was the world crumbling in on him or was he just experiencing a nightmare? If this was a nightmare, it was one he was definitely fighting his hardest to escape.

While he struggled to become free from whatever monster was holding him down, he realized he was being dragged across the sidewalk, his surrounding world still black as night. He could barely make out stifled voices. One? No, two deep voices; definitely, two men. They were discussing how to lift him. But lift him to where? Soon, his question was answered. A large coarse-feeling piece of "something" was abruptly slid between the sidewalk and his backside. With a jolt, he was violently hoisted into the air and dumped into an abyss. A loud slam echoed through his ears and the voices became even more distant.

Fear started coursing through his veins. What was happening? Who did these voices belong to? What did they want with him? Didn't they know he had a very important evening ahead of him with the pooch of his dreams? All of this nonsense was putting him far behind schedule.

The floor of whatever he was laying upon started to rumble and vibrate uncomfortably below his body. He must be in a trunk of a car, he thought frantically. He knew the sound of a car from the many times he had accompanied his master for a jaunt in the country. Oh, how he loved riding in automobiles! His master would roll down the windows and Mermilo would stick his big furry head out the passenger side, feeling the rush of cool wind whipping through his cheeks. His big jowls would rustle against the force of the air, allowing the drool to fly out of his mouth, hopefully not hitting the car behind them, and Mermilo would feel free and fresh.

A good car ride was one of his favorite pastimes. Unfortunately, it certainly wasn't a favorite when he was trapped in the trunk. This space was dark, cramped and very uncomfortable. Oh, how he wished he was in the front seat right now with his master.

The car started moving, but poor Mermilo could not tell which direction he was heading. How could this be happening? The poor retriever was just minding his own business, making his way to get groomed and gussied up for his exciting evening with the poodle of his dreams. Why me? Why?

As he lay in the trunk feeling panicked and forlorn, the car continued to speed further and further away from Mermilo's original destination, towards an unknown location.

Chapter 2

Clausen's Clipper Clinic was bustling that morning and full of excited customers. Terriers, hounds, wiener dogs, Pekingese…pooches of all shapes, sizes and colors were patiently waiting their turn to be made into the beautiful canines of their innermost dreams. Many were regular customers at their regularly scheduled times.

Mermilo had been a devoted client for more than three years, never missing an appointment. In fact, Mermilo was always early.

"Fifteen minutes early is being on time", was his motto. So, when it was ten minutes past his scheduled appointment time, Cheryl, his stylist, became alarmed. That wasn't at all characteristic of the retriever.

"I wonder what could have happened or where he is?" she thought.

From somewhere deep inside her sub-conscience, a tiny voice kept urging her to call his house and find out why he had been delayed. He never missed an appointment. She knew how much he prided himself on his personal hygiene and appearance. She walked over to the counter where the phone was sitting, picked it up, and dialed Mermilo's number. A gentleman answered the phone.

"Hello? This is Stan. Can I help you?"

"Hello Mr. Dudley. This is Cheryl at Clausen's Clipper Clinic. Mermilo had a scheduled grooming appointment today, and he is ten minutes late. I am calling to find out if he is on his way. He is usually early, but he has not shown up yet. That is very unlike him."

"My. That is very unlike him." Mr. Dudley answered, showing concern in his voice. "He is always such a prompt individual. I had better get in the car and search for him. I will let you know what I find out. Thanks so much for calling."

Mr. Dudley carefully hung up the phone. He stood quietly, scratching the back of his head, deep in thought. Mermilo would never make an appointment and not show up without any notice.

Could he have gotten sidetracked? Was it possible he had stopped to talk to a friend? Maybe he had encountered someone who had asked for a hand with a task. Even so, Mermilo would not be late for an appointment.

Still scratching his head, Mr. Dudley quickly grabbed his car keys and his hat off the front hall table, and headed out the door. He had a strange feeling in his stomach that something was not quite right, and he had to get to the bottom of it immediately. Time was of the essence.

Chapter 3

The trunk rattled and shook, tossing Mermilo from side to side. Every muscle in his body ached and the odor of dirt, sweat and gasoline filled his nostrils, making his head throb even more than it already did. Why would someone want to do this to him? He was known in the town as "the gentle giant". Mermilo always went out of his way to help anyone or anything in need.

As a matter of fact, one sunny afternoon a few weeks earlier, the tomcat that lived next door had cornered a small terrified mouse that had been trespassing underneath a rosebush in the dark depths of the cat's backyard. Mermilo, who had been casually waltzing down the street, suddenly heard
desperate cries and pleas for mercy. Naturally, "the gentle giant" gallantly rushed to the scene to administer help to the one in need.

Of course, the cat had not been overly excited to see Mermilo emerge through the back gate. On the other hand, the mouse was thrilled to death (no pun intended). After many minutes of debate and diplomatic discussion as to why mice were full of cholesterol and not a very healthy diet choice for felines, the cat grudgingly agreed to grant the mouse his freedom. The mouse was forever grateful to "the gentle giant". Mermilo, on the other hand, had to pay heavily for his heroic behavior by promising to hand over his juicy beefy-burger bits dinner to the tomcat for the next week, seeing as how he had helped the cat's gourmet meal escape. Oh well. It was definitely worth it, to save the life of a fellow animal friend.

The car turned one direction then another, confusing Mermilo even more as to what direction they were headed the vehicle drove on for what seemed like hours. Well, it seemed like hours when your four legs were bound together, your eyes were covered and you could hardly breathe, let alone being cramped into an uncomfortable, small, smelly, dirty area. Yes, he was pretty sure it had been hours.

All he could think about was that at this very moment some other dog was taking his appointment time. That was unacceptable. He would be a longhaired, smelly, dirty retriever at dinner this evening. The beautiful curly-haired brown-eyed poodle would glare at him in disgust, trying to determine why she had ever agreed to go out with a disgusting mangy mutt like him in the first place. That was not how he wanted the first evening, of possibly the rest of his life, to go. *I have to get out of this predicament, but how? I need a plan and I need one fast.*

Chapter 4

Stan Dudley jumped into his car as fast as lightning, quickly started the car, jammed the gears into reverse, and backed down the driveway. Something was not right and he had to put the pieces of the puzzle together. He shifted the car into drive, and went speeding down the street; his eyes darted right to left, searching for a large golden-colored mass wandering along the sidewalk. Nothing fitting that description could be spotted on his street, so he veered left onto Hazelnut Street, the route that Mermilo most likely would have taken to get to Clausen's Clipper Clinic. So far, Mermilo was nowhere in sight. Panic started to grip Mr. Dudley's stomach. Mermilo was his pride and joy, his companion, his sidekick, his best friend.

They had met four years earlier. Mr. Dudley had decided that a dog would brighten up his life, so he had headed down to the local animal shelter in hopes of finding a true friend and loyal companion.

He had looked at just about every kind of dog imaginable. He had petted miniature schnauzers, large collies, and average sized mutts. He'd snuggled dachshunds and teeny tiny yorkies, but it wasn't until he had come to the last cage in the room that his heart stood still.

Sitting inside, on a bare concrete floor shivering, was a cute cuddly golden retriever puppy. His eyes were drooped with sadness and you could tell by the look on his face his heart ached from loneliness. He had been abandoned by a family that had moved away. The shelter employees weren't quite sure if he had accidentally been left behind, or if he had been forgotten on purpose. Either way, it didn't matter. Mr. Dudley knew as soon as they locked eyes with each other and the pup's tail started to wag that this dog was the one for him.

Mr. Dudley continued driving through town searching for his dear friend, but to no avail. He even stopped and asked some townspeople if they had seen Mermilo earlier this morning. No one could recall spotting the big dog trotting down the street. Mr. Dudley was heartbroken. What direction should he go now? No one had seen him, so he could be anywhere. Sadly, Stan Dudley drove down the street, looking and searching not only with his eyes and ears, but with his heart.

Chapter 5

Mr. Dudley had just driven by when out from behind an old maple tree, a bushy, longhaired, sandy colored feline lazily sauntered out and plopped his fuzzy behind down on the concrete sidewalk.

"Hhmmmmm," he thought to himself. "Interesting. I wonder why everyone is looking for Mermilo? He's not really that fantastic or special. For some reason everyone always seems to think he is. Oh well. Too bad they didn't ask me. I spotted him earlier. He didn't look like he was enjoying himself too much. I wonder what those two burly brutes wanted with him? I guess it's none of my business. If they aren't going to take the time to ask me, I'm not going to waste my breath telling them what I observed. It's too bad for poor old Mermilo."

The cat began meandering slowly down the sidewalk back to his storm sewer. You see, Fats Furball, as he was known on the streets and in the sewer, was a homeless one, with no food nor shelter….nor love from anyone. He relied on himself for everything he needed in life. He had never had a human of his own. He was born wild. His mother had been a cat on the prowl, and this was now his lifestyle, too.

Oh sure, sometimes he wished that some human would take him in, give him shelter and food, and most of all love. Yes, he had several garages in the neighborhood that left their doors up a tad bit so he could squeeze under them to get out of the rain or snow, or escape the heat in the summer. Yet he didn't really have a home to call his very own, with a human to pet his neck, or to curl up on their lap, or to purr to like a jet engine, or to snuggle up with at night at the foot of their bed. No, he was all alone, wandering aimlessly throughout the town's storm pipes and cold barren streets.

Still the last thing he wanted from anyone was pity. In fact, he was a rough, old tomcat who could take care of himself. Come to think of it, he didn't need some mushy, sensitive, emotional human to tie him down. He was free to come and go as he pleased. He had the greatest life! Or, at least that's what he kept telling himself deep down inside.

With that in mind, he surely wasn't going to go out of his way to help some spoiled dog that didn't know the true meaning of survival. No sir. Mermilo was on his own.

"Hmmph."

And with that the old cat was out of sight.

Chapter 6

The car suddenly came to a screeching halt. Mermilo was thrown forward into the trunk. His snout hit the hard wall of the car, causing him to yelp in pain. The mesh material over his head was irritating his cheeks and face, making it very difficult to breath. When was this ordeal going to end? His question would be answered very soon.

The car engine rattled to a stop, sputtered and died. They had arrived at their destination, but where was that? The trunk lid flew open with a loud, heavy creeeak and four hands reached in and grabbed Mermilo around his neck and hindquarters. Whoever these people were, they sure weren't very gentle. They lifted him up and out of the trunk, placing him onto a rocky gravel surface. He struggled to get up onto his four legs, but it was tough work, for they were very weak from the cramped, hot car ride. The sun on his fur was hot and the sweat dripped from his nose into the mesh type bag around his head. *Where were we? What in the world was going on?*

Before he had time to make any sense of it all, he felt a sharp jolt on his neck as he was dragged inside a hot, humid structure, with the mesh material still draped over his muzzle and face so he couldn't see a single thing as he was pulled along. The air was heavy with the smell of cigars, oil and sweat. He knew there was dirt on the ground because he could feel it squish up through the pads of his feet. They stepped over some kind of threshold and into yet another dirt-covered floor. The mesh cover over his head kept it dark, but as he was led further into his jail, the darkness became more intense under his mask.

The men's voices were grumbling to each other and out of nowhere, the bag covering Mermilo's head was ripped off with sheer force. It yanked his neck sideways in an unusual manner, again causing him to yelp out in pain. He was kicked in the backside and shoved into a huge kennel, much like the one Mr. Dudley had found him in at the pound. But this time, there were six other dogs in the kennel with him.

What was this place? Something suspicious was going on; suspicious in an eerie way that gave Mermilo a very *bad* feeling. Why were all these other dogs here? Had the same thing happened to them? There was only one way to find out. But he would have to wait until he had a safe opportunity to talk to them. Right now the men were standing in front of the kennel, looking them up and down.

"Hey Roy, did I ever tell ya' I hate mutts? They smell, and they are useless creatures. They ain't got no purpose in life."

"Ah, come on, Shep. When I was a boy, we had a dog. His name was Ryder; a huge dog he was. Hmmmmm, come to think of it, he did always have a somewhat sickening smell about him. Yours truly here always had to feed him twice a day, fetch him fresh water, clean up his doo-doo in the yard, comb his matted fur, make sure he was let into the house at night…what a royal pain that was. I didn't even want him in the first place. My brother brought him home without asking the folks. They were not happy with him. Gosh, after thinking about it, I guess I hate mutts, too. They truly are useless animals. That dog didn't do one thing for me. I did everything for him. So… what do you think Henry is going to do with all these pooches? If I had to collect anything, it sure wouldn't be pooches. It'd be MONEY."

"Hey doofus, he's not collecting pooches. He IS collecting money. He's going to sell these mutts on the black market. Haven't you noticed he's got the top breeds of dogs in here? You've got that long-haired Chihuahua, the Afghan hound, the Russian wolf hound, the Siberian husky, the Greyhound, and now that golden retriever. The wolfhound, Afghan hound and retriever will bring him the most mullah. Too bad we gotta figure out what to do with that old Bassett hound, though. He won't bring us anything. He was a sheer waste of time. And geez, was he heavy. Had we known he was that old we could have put our energy into finding a more valuable mutt. But as for the others, we get a third of that dough, Roy. Didn't you know that? The more top breed mutts we collect, the more mullah we get. Where's your brain, man? We aren't doing this just for the fun of it, you know."

"Boys, lock up. We are done here for today." hollered Henry, their boss. He was the head of the whole dog kidnapping operation.

"We need to do some more scouting. I just got word that on the east side of town several Lhasa Apsos and a chocolate lab were sighted. Those go for big bucks. So, quit goofing around. Get this place locked up and get your hides in the car. I'm giving you five minutes or I leave without you and you don't get a cut of the profit. Now move."

Immediately the two thugs made sure Mermilo was securely in the kennel, the door shut tight, then dashed out the entrance of the dimly lit structure yelling for Henry to wait up for them. Mermilo heard the sound of car doors slamming shut and the roar of the motor starting. The noise instantly faded into the distance as the car disappeared down the road.

It was very quiet in the kennel. Mermilo turned around and noticed that the other six dogs were staring at him. He wasn't quite sure what to say or whom to say it to. He didn't have to wonder much longer. The Russian wolf hound quietly stepped forward and began to speak in his Russian-accented voice.

"May I ask who you vould be?", his accent rolling off his tongue with sheer elegance and a husky tone like no other Mermilo had ever heard before.

Mermilo gulped and replied, "My name is Mermilo. I am not quite sure why I am here. I was hoping maybe you could help me figure that out."

"Vell comrade, ve are not quite sure either. Ve all ended up here against our own vills. All of us vere blindfolded, tied up, thrown into the back of a car and now ve are all standing here together. That is about all ve know other than they are planning to get rid of us somehow. And by the vay, my name is Vlad."

Mermilo thought quietly for a moment. He wasn't about to let that happen if he could help it. He had a big date tonight and he wasn't going to miss it. Not after how long it took him to make it happen.

He sat down on the dirt floor and started to think. He knew they would have to work together as a team if they wanted to bust out of here. He slowly stood up, cleared his throat, and spoke directly to Vlad.

"I'm not quite sure why you or I or any of us, for that matter, are here. Still what I do know is that we need to get out of here, and as soon as possible. The problem is I'm not quite certain how we can do it though I am trying to figure that out. If we are to work together to free ourselves, we first must know each other's names. As I said earlier, I am Mermilo. It's nice to meet you. I wish it were under different circumstances but, unfortunately, it is not."

Vlad nodded silently and turned to the rest of the group.

"Quiet. Quiet please. I vant you all to meet Mermilo. He is their newest addition to the group. Fortunately, Mermilo thinks he may be able to help us escape and get back to our masters and homes. Mermilo, vat did you have in mind?"

Mermilo hesitated, then replied, "I am not exactly sure. I was hoping maybe you could fill me in on how they run things around here."

"Ahhhh cheewahwah.", chimed in the Chihuahua. "I see everything senor. I watch them closely. They come in like trains, sound like earthquakes, make much commotion, talk loudly, bring dogs…aaahhhh, I see everything. They are a lazy pair. They sit in their chairs and sleep a lot. Glad to meet you. My name is Chico."

The little dog jumped up and flipped around several times. His long hair and scraggly tail were flying through the air like a circus acrobat on a trapeze. The little mutt was so excited that finally he might be able to do something for someone - even if it was to be only the eyes of the operation. A dog his size wasn't known for being a big strong hero. He was more like a tiny throw rug, or longhaired rat, as some people referred to him.

Why, just a few days ago, he had been on his leash happily prancing down the street with his human. They were strolling along quite quickly, enjoying their morning jaunt when she tossed a little doggie treat into the air for him to enjoy. He always received several during their daily strolls for walking so mannerly on his leash.

Sadly, the tidbit hit his small jowl and bounced off onto the sidewalk. It continued rolling, plopping onto the street's storm grate, and cascading down through the steel bars. Chico was so distraught to lose his treat that he tried to crawl down into the drain to retrieve his snack.

His owner, a small girl, was struggling to keep hold of his leash. Chico was so petite that he very easily could have fallen right through the grates, which he almost did. Luckily, she had a tight grasp. As he tried to jump down between the bars, she fell to the sidewalk, grabbing him just in the nick of time.

At that moment, an older woman was approaching from behind, and as the young girl stood up and turned around, the only thing the woman could see was a wildly kicking tiny furry ball in the girl's arms. This tiny furry ball had four skinny legs and a scraggly tail. The woman immediately started screaming.

"Sewer rat. Sewer rat. Let it go—it will bite you. Someone help this poor little girl. She's being attacked by a disgusting sewer rat."

At that, the woman immediately took her umbrella and started whacking poor Chico over his little tiny head. The girl, frantically trying to shield her beloved Chihuahua, hollered that it was her dog and to leave him alone. But the woman was so distraught over the thought of a rat in the girl's arms that she continued with her tantrum. Chico's owner tried her hardest to barricade him from the violent blows by turning her back to the irate woman and cradling Chico against her chest, but alas…by the time it all ended, poor Chico's head felt like a flattened tortilla. What a headache the poor little dog had. They eventually escaped the wrath of the passerby, but poor Chico would never forget it.

Chico began to yip excitedly all the information he could give about his own situation and how he had ended up in this place. He had been in his backyard taking his evening "break" before dinner, when out of nowhere two grizzly looking guys appeared standing next to him. *How did they get into my backyard? What do they want?*

"Intruders." Chico yelped to his owners in his loudest Chihuahua voice. But no one heard him. They were all inside busily chatting while preparing dinner. No one was paying any attention to Chico in the backyard.

Chico continued yelping in his high-pitched bark, but it was futile. Four rough hands grasped his tiny furry body and he was suddenly whisked up into the air and tossed into some sort of bag. His yelping continued throughout the whole escapade, but unfortunately the bag muffled most of his sound. He was rushed out of the yard through the unlocked back gate and tossed into a trunk with a thud that rattled every little bone in his body. With a loud slam over his head as the trunk lid was being shut, the engine of the car started vibrating underneath the little dog, and he could feel himself being driven away to some unknown destination. The bumping and rattling made the little dog extremely uncomfortable; especially since he had not been able to take his evening "break".

But now it was *his* turn to be able to help someone in need. He could hardly wait. Mermilo thanked him for his information and made a mental note to himself…*Chico would be a great lookout.*

Next, up stepped the Afghan hound. Her long lustrous silky blond coat swayed gently side to side as she made her way forward through the group. In her deepest, huskiest voice she proceeded to introduce herself.

"Well, hello Mermilo. My name is Queenie. I am quite a beautiful sight, don't you think? Is this escape operation going to cause any harm or damage to my velvety flowing fur? I certainly hope not. It takes forever to comb out and unfortunately, I do not have my comb with me. Nor do I have my lipstick, hairspray or mascara. Those thugs showed up without any warning and, in all the excitement, I dropped my purse containing my beauty essentials. Thank goodness my fur had just been styled! I was leaving the salon when they appeared out of nowhere and grabbed me. Naturally I did the sensible thing and went without a fuss, so as not to mess my exotic flowing fur. I would be horrified to be dognapped with my fur a mess. Could you imagine? Do you notice how it almost touches the floor in a dramatic cascading manner? Any sudden movement causes tangles that are nearly impossible to comb out. That's why I try to be poised and still most of the time. Still I also feel I look the most beautiful that way. Don't you agree? I will try to help in any way that I can as long as it's not too messy or involved."

She batted her long silky eyelashes at him and smiled the most dazzling canine smile she could manage.

Mermilo nodded, blinked his eyes, and made another mental note—*use Queenie for a decoy; very pretty, but more than likely useless in any other position.*

Queenie slowly sashayed back to her spot in the kennel. It was now the large heavy Bassett hound's turn to identify himself. He had an oversized load to carry and was struggling to make his way up to Mermilo. Finally, he stood in front of the retriever, plopped his big bottom down, and turned his face upward to look at the golden mass of soft flowing fur. In his slow deep bassett hound voice he began to introduce himself.

Helloooo. My name is Beauregaaard. How are you doing?"

Mermilo slowly smiled and nodded politely to the old fellow. You could tell he was old just by looking at him. His skin wrinkled in more folds than a newly laundered bed sheet, his teeth were a deep dingy yellow and some were missing all together, his ears were furless in certain areas, and his voice was low, slow, and very hard to get out of his throat. Yep, this dog had seen many days. Mermilo had no idea how old he was, but could pretty well surmise that he was well beyond his expected years.

Old Beauregard was just hanging on by a tooth. But you would never have suspected that by listening to him speak. I mean, his mental state was that of a young pup.

"I know they are hitting the whooooole town, looking for all types of dogs. I was minding my ooooown business, grabbing a beagle bite burger when out of nowhere this thing came down on my head. Well, I certainly wasn't expecting that, so of course, I just lay down. I'm too ooooold to fight. I was ready for a rest anyway, so I didn't give them any trouble. The worst part was that car ride. It did a number on my ooold bones. I'm so sore I can hardly get around. But I'm here to help you in any way possible. I *can* tell you this…I am ready to go hooome. I am an old man. I need my orthopedic pillow. Oh, one more thing that you may want to know. It was an old red fooouuuur door car that they dumped me in. I happened to spot it as I was unwrapping my burger. The two men were heavyset gents; one was sporting a gray beard and the other one was bald. I ignored them because I just assumed they were ordering burgers, too. Does that help ya any, sonny?"

Mermilo was so thankful for any piece of information he could get.

"Thank you Beauregard. I truly appreciate the input."

The old dog smiled his yellow semi-toothless grin, slowly picked his carcass up off the ground, and meandered back to where he was laying. Just that small feat alone tuckered the old feller out. He plumped down and immediately started snoring.

Mermilo was beginning to realize that these dogs wanted to go home as much as he did. He wondered if they had as an important evening ahead of them as he did. He was starting to hope deep in his heart that he would make it to his date tonight. He was beginning to panic.

Chapter 7

Fats Furball crawled down in through the storm sewer grate and wandered along towards his home. The sewer was a dark, damp place with very little, if any, sunlight. There was dirt, grime and mud everywhere. Fats was never a clean kitty due to his living conditions, but he was a fluffy ball of fur so full and round that when you looked at him, you knew that given a little spit and shine, he'd be a handsome tan and white long-haired feline God. But no one had ever thought to give him that kind of attention, so he remained the dirty, furry fuzzball that he was.

He made his way over dead branches, rocks, and strewn trash that had managed to flow down through the sewer. He turned along a sharp bend in the pipes and headed straight towards his home—his newspaper and a dirty old chair cushion that one day had miraculously appeared.

It had been a cold, snowy night sometime last winter and Fats was trying to cuddle down into a huge stack of wet newspaper; when suddenly out of nowhere, a tattered, old chair cushion came tumbling down the pipe towards his roost. He quickly pounced on it before it could roll on by and eagerly hauled it into his corner.

Kitty heaven was definitely looking out for him. He had truly believed that night, as cold as the temperatures had fallen, that he would probably not make it through to the morning without freezing to death. While thinking that thought, the cushion appeared out of thin air. It truly was a miracle. He lay down on his new soft mattress and bundled up some of the newspaper so it covered him like a blanket. He snuggled in for a much needed long night's rest. That blustery evening was as peaceful and warm as if he were sleeping on a down-filled comforter on some over-sized bed in a king's castle.

Yes, someone was truly looking out for him. He suddenly felt as if someday his luck would change for the better. But until then, he had to keep doing what he was doing…surviving.

He curled up on his cushioned bed, and nibbled a small bite from a piece of dried up cheese he had found in the park. Cheese was one of his favorites. He didn't come across it very often, but when he did, his whole day was spectacular. The cheese of course, would be extremely hard and most of the flavor would be lacking. It still took extra chewing time to be able to swallow it, which made it seem like a much larger meal than it actually was.

Fats was familiar with the fact that cheese is a favorite snack of mice. He would purposefully sleep with his mouth open, making sure to take deep breaths of air and puff out that cheesy-smelling breath as hard as he could. Maybe, if there was a mouse nearby, he would smell the stale stinky aroma and come to investigate. It had only worked once, and it had made for a delightful holiday dinner—even if it wasn't the holidays.

He settled himself in for his noon nap. He lay on his bed getting drowsy, recalling the events of this morning.

"What in the world did those men want with Mermilo? And why would they cover his head and throw him in a trunk? I don't know but I'm too tired to think about it. It almost seems…

zzz…

like the same thing I saw over on…

zzz…

Pepperidge Street yesterday…

zzz….huh?"

All at once, Fats was wide-awake. To make sure he was alert and not sleepwalking, he took another bite of hard cheese. The somewhat cheesy cardboard flavor was coming through in his mouth loud and clear. He was definitely awake.

Holy cow. What was going on here, he thought? He remembered seeing two guys taking that Bassett hound the other day, the poor fellow. He was so old and tired. He was just trying to enjoy his burger. Fats had to give him credit, though. Even as the burly dudes ambushed him, the Bassett hound just kept chomping away at his meal.

Fats no longer felt the need to nap. His mind was racing erratically and his emotions were raw. His thoughts pulsated in his brain as he tried to figure out what to do next. Who should he alert about the situation? What could he possibly do to help them? This was a serious matter that was weighing heavily on his conscience.

How could he have felt so cold and apathetic towards Mermilo? The poor dog was just walking down the street minding his own business.

"Oh dear, oh dear. I need to get out of here and do something to help."

With that, Fats threw off his newspaper covers and leaped off his cushion, bounded back through the pipes and up onto the street into the noonday sunlight. He took off like he had been shot out of a cannon, heading to where he knew he could get the assistance he required.

Chapter 8

Stan Dudley pulled into the parking lot of Clausen's Clipper Clinic. Heart racing, he opened his door and headed directly to the entrance of the salon. Pooches of all breeds were filing in and out of the establishment. This was the only hair design business in the entire town that catered strictly to canines and felines, so it was a constant madhouse of clientele.

It had been built thirty years earlier by a rich, elderly gentleman named Claude Arel Clausen, who had created it for his three beautiful black Labrador dogs. His dogs had been the love of his life after his wife of forty years had passed away. His world revolved around them. He did anything and everything to make their lives comfortable and lush. They were his children.

He had hired the most reknown dog groomer in the world, Sir Charles Cutsalot, from Great Britain. He was known worldwide for his immaculate precise groomings and eccentric stylings. His expertise of fashionable combing, shampooing, manicuring of nails, conditioning of coats and exquisite teeth whitening made him highly requested among the royalty of many countries.

The salon was so famous and successful that it continued doing an exorbitant amount of business even after the elderly Clausen's death. He had generously left the salon to the town council in his will, as long as they continued to assure its amenities would always remain available to the general public.

Even after Sir Cutsalot had passed away, his children took over as head groomers and stylists. Cheryl was actually the granddaughter of Sir Cutsalot, and she took her profession just as seriously as her grandfather had throughout his many years as a professional stylist. Mermilo was her most loyal and favorite customer, and had been for several years. She knew him well.

Stan entered the front door and Cheryl immediately came over to him.

"Did you find him?" she asked.

"No. I was hoping he had appeared here in the meantime. Apparently he hasn't. Cheryl, I have a very bad feeling about this. It is so uncharacteristic of him to miss a grooming appointment, especially with his big night tonight! I can't even imagine where he could possibly be. I have no choice but to go to the police."

"That would be a wise thing to do. I have been hearing rumors all morning about other dogs around town that have suddenly gone missing in the past few days. There is a Russian wolf hound over on Mammoth Road that suddenly disappeared off his front porch on Monday afternoon. And someone else mentioned a tiny Chihuahua that didn't appear when he was called in from his backyard for dinner. He had simply vanished into thin air. Something is very suspicious. We need to get to the bottom of it—for Mermilo's sake." Cheryl replied anxiously.

Stan thought about it for a few moments. He turned to head out the front door and swung back around to face Cheryl.

"If you see him, please call me immediately. I will not rest until I find my best friend."

And with that, he was out the door, in his car and already halfway down the street before Cheryl could even respond.

Chapter 9

As the Bassett hound lay snoring loudly on the dirt floor, a massive ball of thick gray and white fur approached Mermilo. The Siberian husky made his way forward through the dogs to introduce himself to the retriever and asked what he could do to help. As he approached, Mermilo stared at him inquisitively.

"This dog looks familiar. Where do I know him from?" he mentally asked himself.

The husky grinned a big sharp-toothed grin, his icy pale blue eyes flickering in the dim light.

"Hey. Nice to meet you Mermilo." he said. "Sorry you are in the same mess we are. The gang here is really confused about what they want with us. Vlad and I have been trying to figure that out and somehow devise a plan to stop them. By the way, my name is Mookha."

Mermilo nodded and returned the smile.

"Thanks, Mookha." Mermilo replied. "Like I said, we need to work together as a team to get everyone out of here alive. Can you tell me anything?"

"Well, I was in the park with my master, training for the upcoming sled pull that is being held a few weeks away in the northern mountains. Tim, my owner, had just unleashed me from the sled and was putting our equipment back into the trailer. I had taken a trot out into the field to, well, take care of some "dog" business, if you know what I mean. When I had finished I was heading back to the truck and heard something rustle in the bushes at the edge of the park. I turned around to look and realized that something or someone seemed to be in trouble. So naturally, being the goodhearted, not to mention handsome fellow that I am, I trotted over to investigate. Up north, I'm always rescuing little squirrels, rabbits and birds from bushes and vines. So, I just assumed it was something of the same nature. Boy was that the furthest thing from the truth.

I entered the bushes and as I was sticking my snout into a small clearing underneath a shrub to investigate, something came down over my head. It was like a mesh type material, connected to a long pole; a net of some sort. A leash was quickly hooked onto my collar, and my front and hind legs were grabbed and abruptly yanked out from beneath me. I fell with a thud onto my backside and I was dragged through the bushes and briars. I couldn't even make a sound to alert Tim.

I remember being picked up by someone, and thrown into a small dark container of sorts. It sure knocked the wind out of me, and I don't admit that to too many people. Seriously, a huge Siberian husky like myself getting knocked to the ground by a net? Nope, I tend to keep those kinds of things to myself."

Mookha shrugged his shoulders as he had nothing else to add. Mermilo thanked him and Mookha proudly strutted back to his spot in the kennel. Mental note—*use that guy where strength is needed.*

As Mermilo watched him stroll away, he realized how he knew that dog. His picture was everywhere around town during the winter months. He was famous! Mookha was a member of an elite sled team—Ice Team Twenty, named after the age of his owner when the team formed, and because they raced on snow and ice. His team had actually won the Alaskan Iditarod Dogsled Race a few years back and they were practicing to win it again. Mermilo knew he had known him from somewhere, and now he was relieved that he had finally figured it out.

The air was getting warm and musty inside the structure. The midday sun was directly overhead, beating down upon the shelter. The smell of dirt and sweat was becoming increasingly heavy in the air. And of course, the thieves had left without supplying water to any of the poor prisoners. They needed to come up with a plan and fast. If the thugs didn't do them in, thirst and heat exhaustion surely would.

Chapter 10

Fats Furball raced down the street, searching for his buddy Purina. The two were great friends. The only difference between them was Purina had a home and an owner; Fats had a storm sewer and a newspaper covered cushion. Purina was loved by a family. Fats ate hard cheese. Purina was clean and groomed. Fats was filthy, smelly, and matted.

Yet that didn't matter to the two friends. In fact, sometimes when the nights were warm, Purina would prop open one of the loose slats in the privacy fence of his backyard, allowing Fats to sneak in after everyone in the house had gone to bed. There on the patio, Fats would curl up on the family's nice wicker chair and dream the night away. Purina would always make sure on those heavenly nights to leave him a little stash of dry cat food to enhance his evening pleasure. Yes, one could say they were the best of friends and would do anything to help each other.

They had met several years earlier when Fats wandered into Purina's front yard. Purina had been napping soundly on his front stoop, when suddenly he smelled the presence of another feline on his turf. Purina immediately snapped to alertness and, of course, had entered into the common tough guy cat-mode: hunched back, spiked-up fur, menacing growls coming from deep within his throat, and naturally the good old "come and get me" fur ball spits.

Fats, of course, had immediately hacked back another spit-filled fur ball and the war was on. They hissed and hunched and initiated a fancy cat-type dance resulting in circular strides that covered the front lawn. After a few moments of this performance, Fats realized this was utter nonsense, so he deflated himself back down to his normal size, apologized and turned to leave Purina's territory. Watching the intruder walk away, Purina suddenly felt awkwardly foolish.

"Wait." Purina yelled, not realizing until after he had said it that it came out of his mouth.

What was the big deal that another cat had wandered onto his lawn? It was his lawn and it wasn't as if this cat was trying to stake a legal claim. This was the property of Purina's owners. So, what was his personal hang-up? He lowered his head and pondered for a few moments, searching through his thoughts.

Purina looked back up just as Fats was turning around to sit down comfortably on the lawn, his bottom situated between several patches of high grass. The intruder was contentedly staring at him, waiting for Purina to say something.

This was not like himself, Purina thought. He was normally a feline that strived to help others in need, or at least he felt he was. Why was he acting in this manner? Had he become one of those "tom" cats around town, trying to be a big man? He deeply and sincerely hoped he had not become that sort of cat!

The two struck up a civil conversation. Purina let all his defenses down, and realized he and Fats truly had a lot in common. They discussed their favorite hobbies, their distaste for the canine species, their favorite flavor of rodents, and other various topics. It was that day the bond between the two best friends was formed, and it has been in place ever since.

Now Fats really needed his buddy's help. He dashed down the street, scurried across the lawn, darted through the hole in the backyard fence, and hurried up to the patio. Purina was curled up into a ball on the hammock, taking his early afternoon snooze. He was so deep in slumber he did not even hear his friend approaching.

"Purina, wake up. I need your help. There is something funny going on in town. Wake up." Fats hollered at his friend.

Purina slowly started to stir. His nice dream of dining on grilled mice and shallots was suddenly over. Ah man….he was just putting the forkful of tasty morsels into his mouth.

"Fats, this had better be pretty important, for your sake. I've never had mice and shallots; and I was about to experience it for the first time." Purina responded without even opening his eyes.

"Oh buddy, this is important. It's really important. There is something very weird happening. Our animal friends are slowly and suspiciously vanishing into thin air. I don't like the smell of this," Fats answered.

"I don't like the smell of some of our animal friends to begin with, so what's the big deal?" Purina responded.

"That's not what I mean. I mean they are disappearing right out from under our noses. Someone is taking them, Purina. I have a feeling that whatever they want with them, it's not good. We need to find out who and why if we want to help our canine counterparts."

"And just why would we want to help a dog? They don't care for us and we don't care for them either. Life would be grand without any dogs around. Don't you think? No drooling, no slobbering, no shaking their wet gross furry bodies, no clumps of you know what laying around in the yard, no annoying whining or barking….I'm not seeing the advantage of helping those nuisances," Purina slowly replied.

Fats wrinkled his face in disbelief. "Purina, life would not be the same without dogs. They protect us, they scare larger enemies away, and quite frankly, you should be thankful you have a dog in your house. He takes all the excessive attention off of you. Do you really want to be petted, touched and mauled twenty-four hours a day, seven days a week? You wouldn't even be able to use the litter box privately. They'd be standing right outside your door waiting for you to exit so they could scoop you up again and continue with their personal space invasion—right where they had left off. Don't you like a little alone time? Like right now? You're out here enjoying your midday nap and your family's dog is inside providing entertainment to your humans, allowing you the opportunity to experience some peace and quiet. I am watching him right now through the window as we speak. They are making him do those ridiculous pet tricks again….sit, beg, shake…it's humiliating .If it weren't for him, they'd be out here carting you around. You would never be able to get your beauty rest. Think about it carefully, Purina. Be extremely careful what you wish for!"

Purina pondered all this information, slowly deciding if Fats had a good point. After several minutes of thought, and watching the family dog through the window as he made a complete idiot of himself, Purina was one hundred percent on board with the idea of solving the case of the missing dogs.

"OK, I'm in. Let's do this. I can't bear the thought of having to do all of the boloney that they put that poor dog through. Wow, and I thought dogs were smart. What a clown."

Within seconds, the two were out the fence, across the yard, and bounding down the street towards midtown. The first stop would be the sidewalk where Mermilo was last seen. Maybe there would be clues that they could use.

Chapter 11

The dogs were really starting to feel the brunt of the midday heat by now. They were heaped throughout the kennel upon the dirty floor, wishing for a bowl of cold crystal clear water. Mermilo was trying his best to stay calm and keep a cool head. While sitting there deep in thought, the greyhound approached him quietly.

He was a sleek, deep velvety gray color, muscles rippling as he walked, his poise and demeanor that of a true winner. He gracefully moved forward through the group and stopped right in front of Mermilo. He sat down, eyed Mermilo up and down and began to speak slowly and quietly. "My name is Dolph Charlinn Maxwell. That is my full name given at birth, as I am a purebred greyhound. You can call me Max for short. I am not trying to sound harsh or rude, but I really must get out of here. I have a very important event to attend this evening. It is for an extremely urgent cause and I mustn't let them down."

Mermilo definitely knew the meaning of "an extremely urgent" event, as he also had one this evening.

"I will do my best to help us all. Can you tell me anything about how you ended up here?"

Max thought for a moment before continuing.

"Well, I was at the dog track practicing my graceful race moves, minding my own business. My owner had let me loose to work on my own. You see, the track is surrounded by fences, so there was no way I could wander off, as if I would even want to. I was practicing my take-offs and turnabouts, as I am performing for the children's hospital this evening. I used to race professionally. But due to a torn ankle tendon, I had to retire. My owner thought that as successful as I was at racing, I may be as big of a success at helping others. So, I was selected as the official mascot for the Metropolitan Children's Hospital, and I perform there three times a week. Tonight is a public fundraiser. The money will be spent on research for cures of terminal illnesses that strike children. I simply must be there.

Mermilo cocked his head and looked at Max curiously.

"I am sorry, I am digressing. Yes, yes, back to the bad guys. I was practicing, as I said earlier, and stopped for a breather. I decided to trot over to the watershed to replenish my hydration. As I was sipping some refreshing water, out of nowhere a device encapsulated my head and neck. I nearly choked to death. I was extremely alarmed as I didn't know what was happening. I did not resist, because of my torn tendon and I did not want to injure it further. So, I stood quite still, hoping whatever or whomever it was would disappear. Unfortunately, they didn't. To my displeasure, they were rather rough with me.

They grabbed my torso, yanked my delicate legs together, and dragged me off the track. The friction wore a tender area on my left side. Can you see it there?" He turned to allow Mermilo to peek at his wound.

Mermilo studied it carefully and replied, "I am so sorry to hear that, Max."

"Yes, I as well," Max responded.

"As I was saying, they dragged me off the track, lifted me up—I seem to remember feeling four hands- and they tossed me into the trunk of a car. The reason I knew that was because I could see a slit of light from beneath the net and I could see four feet, the dirt ground, and the back end of the car. In fact, I also remember seeing that it was a red car and it had a license plate."

Max stood there drifting off into deep thought. Mermilo took immediate attention to the words "license plate".

"Max, did you get a good look at the plate? Could you tell me the license plate numbers? This could be a huge break for us all. Think. Close your eyes and picture the back end of the car.

Max slowly closed his eyes and thought quietly. "Yes, yes I see it. FBH348…no, 9. FBH349 definitely. I remember the plate because I quickly thought, in my panicked mind, how appropriate that I was being accosted by a car with this license plate number. 'Four Big Hands' that grabbed me and it was approximately 3:49 in the afternoon. Rather fitting for the situation, wouldn't you say?"

Mermilo acknowledged his connection, thinking nothing at this moment was fitting for their situation. Yet he kept his thoughts to himself.

"Thanks so much, Max. This may be the big break that we need to get us all out of here."

Vlad stepped forward.

"But Mermilo, how are ve going to let anyone know the license plate number? How can ve possibly get the vord out?"

Mermilo was thinking the same thing. Yes, they knew the license plate number but what good was this information doing them when they were still locked up in the kennel? They would
have to think hard and quick if they were to get the word out as to their whereabouts.

Chapter 12

Fats and Purina raced down the sidewalk, approaching the exact spot that Mermilo disappeared. Both felines stopped and sat down, panting heavily.

"This is where I saw it all happen. Poor Mermilo didn't know what was coming. It's funny, now that I think back on it. I had been sitting in the Jones' lawn right over there, basking in the morning sun. That's where I usually take my morning rest. There's a nest of rodents under their rosebush, so every now and then I am able to catch a midmorning snack. No such luck today. Anyway, I had noticed several times this week an old red car parked on the other side of the road. There were two guys in it, just sitting, watching, almost like they were waiting for someone. Or something. Now I realize it was Mermilo they were waiting for. They've been watching him all week, so they knew exactly where he walked every morning and at what time he would be appearing on this sidewalk. Stalkers," Fats exclaimed.

Purina sat there thinking.

"Wow. Why would anyone stalk Mermilo? What in the world would they want with him? He's just a smelly dog with big ears and a bushy tail. What's so great about that?" he asked Fats.

"Don't you see what's happening? Mermilo is a purebred Golden Retriever. All the dogs that are missing are purebreds. It's a dog theft ring. I bet they are going to sell them and make money and those poor dogs will never see their homes or masters again. Purina, we've got to do something about this.

"Can you remember anything else about the car? Any dents, hubcaps missing, license plate number?" Purina inquired.

"Holy cow. I saw the plate. Purina, I saw the plate number. I remember it. Let's head over to the police station. Maybe old Roscoe can help us out. He always knows the news of the town. He listens to the officers all the time. There are always good stories when you sit down with Roscoe. Let's go!" Fats demanded.

The two felines bounded down the street in the direction of the town police station to talk to the old tomcat that took up residence there.

Chapter 13

The dogs were deep in thought when they heard the rattle of the car thumping back down the dusty road, approaching the structure. The thieves were back. Already? They weren't gone that long. Car doors opening and shutting were heard from inside the kennel. There seemed to be some commotion as they approached the building.

"Hang on him, Roy. He's a tough one. Wow. He's one heck of a huge Labrador. This one will bring a pretty penny to the pot."

"Shep, he's too heavy. Man, what's this dog been eating. Steak and pizza? He is BIG. And he's got a mean streak to him. I'm not digging this pooch. Drop him in the kennel quick, Roy, and shut the gate. He could be a man-eater."

The two men opened the door, threw the lab inside and quickly slammed the door shut. The rattle of metal filled the air as the door vibrated from the harshness of the closing.

"Phew, that was close. I don't get hazard pay for this job. Some of these dogs scare me." Roy complained.

Shep grunted in agreement.

"Yeah, but think about our paycheck when we finish the job. Man, this is the best job in the world, don't ya' think, Roy?"

"I don't know about the "best job" part, but the pay will be nice. Haha." Roy chimed.

The two men turned their backs on the kennel and started talking between themselves. They headed over an old wooden desk and sat down. Roy leaned back, reached in an old rickety refrigerator sitting behind him, and pulled out a pitcher. Shep gathered two glasses off the shelf next to him and pulled them onto the table. They poured themselves a cold beverage of some sort, slumped back in their creaky wooden chairs, and flipped on an old television set. A western movie was playing and the two of them turned their full attention to that. Before too long, the two were sawing logs, snoring louder than the sound of guns and horses blaring from the television.

Mermilo watched them closely. He needed to make sure they were soundly asleep. What the other dogs didn't realize is that when they had thrown the lab into the kennel and slammed the door shut, neither of the men had locked it. It was unlocked but securely closed, so they hadn't realized they had forgotten. They had been preoccupied by the thought of the Labrador turning on them and giving them a fight.

Still Mermilo was well aware of their mistake. He quietly summoned the other dogs to gather around. He addressed the newest member of the stolen group first. He turned to the Labrador and began to speak in a quiet tone, as not to wake the thugs.

"Hi. My name is Mermilo. This is Vlad, Max, Mookha, Queenie, Chico, and Bulregard."

"I'm Thor," the Labrador replied in a hesitant tone. "What in the world is going on? I am extremely confused. And I dare say a little frightened. I was in the park playing fetch with my master. He tossed a good high lob with my tennis ball that went right over my head, so I ran into a thicket to retrieve it, and BAM. I was grabbed from behind, legs tied, head covered with some kind of bag, and thrown into a trunk. Now I'm here. Where *is* here?"

"We aren't quite sure," Mermilo continued. "I can't explain much right now. We've got to move fast. When they threw you in here, they failed to remember to lock the door. Lady and gentlemen, that door is unlocked as I speak. We have got to move fast before they wake up and realize what is going on."

The dogs all huddled together to devise a plan – a plan that would bust them out of there and get them all back home.

Chapter 14

The two racing cats rounded the corner onto Harbald Avenue and skittered along the sidewalk to the police station. They quickly entered the open basement window, as they always did when they visited old Roscoe, and made their way over to the hole in the wall. They stuffed their furry bodies inside and quickly crawled their way up to the main floor. These two had been there many times before and knew the exact path to take, so it took them only a matter of seconds to make their way out of an opening in the drywall underneath a conference table in the police meeting room.

Old Roscoe was sound asleep on a soft plush pillow in the corner, behind some cardboard boxes stuffed full of office supplies. Roscoe was purring soundly when the two friends pounced upon him.

"Psssst, Roscoe, Roscoe. Wake up. Psssst," Fats hissed quietly.

The old tom slowly stirred in his sleep, licked his paw lazily, rolled over and went right back to snoozing. Fats had no other choice than to stick his paw out, nails slightly extended for effect, and bat him across his face. Roscoe was not one to take that from another tomcat, and Fats knew it. But he had no other choice in this dilemma. He had to get Roscoe awake.

The old shorthaired calico feline slowly started to come-to, making it quite known he was not very happy to be awakened so abruptly. He slowly opened one eye, then the other, yawned such a yawn that you could see all the way down his throat, scratched his ear with his back paw, and threateningly muttered to the two cats standing there staring at him.

"What in tarnation do you two think you are doing coming in here and denying me of my much needed sleep? You sure have got a lot of nerve. Now, spit it out. How come?"

Fats was the first to speak, frantically trying to get Roscoe wide eyed and alert so he could understand every word Fats was about to say.

"Roscoe, we need your help. Something terrible is going on in town, and I think it's only going to get worse if we don't do something. Dogs—they're disappearing everywhere - right from under our noses."

Roscoe scratched his head with his front paw, yawned again, and replied rather slowly and in a confused manner.

"And you are saying this is a problem? I'm not fully understanding your predicament. Dogs, you say? We dislike dogs, don't we? Why is this a problem?"

Roscoe stretched out his hind leg and began licking between his toes. Purina was the one to jump in this time.

"Roscoe, listen. Dogs aren't really our friends, but we need them; for the sake of our feline species. They take a lot of unwanted attention off of us. Fats here had to point that out to me earlier this morning. If you could have only seen what a fool the dog at my house was making of himself in front of the humans. I felt embarrassed for him. I was just grateful it was him and not me they were badgering. It made me shudder inside to think of them hugging me and kissing me and petting me and making me jump in circles for my dinner...*yuck*. Thanks to Fats here, I see now that. We've got to do something or we cats will be in dire trouble."

Roscoe considered this bit of information for several moments. In fact, quite a few long moments before sputtering out an answer.

"Come to think of it, I did hear the Sarge talking to someone on the phone about a missing Greyhound. From the sounds of it, I guess he was a pretty important dog. OK youngin's, fill me in. What's going on?" Roscoe inquired.

It took several minutes of excited gestures, meowing and hissing to get the full story told. But once it came out that the license plate numbers were known, Ol' Roscoe went straight to work. He pulled himself up, dashed across the floor and out the doorway, and headed straight to the sergeant's office.

He bounced up on top of the desk and started rubbing his furry body up against the Sarge's arm. Around and around he went, rubbing one side, turning, then rubbing the other side, with his long calico tail straight in the air, meowing in his sorrowful little way. Sarge was in the middle of typing a police report, but whenever Roscoe jumped up on the desktop, Sarge would always make time for a quick pet and scratch under the chin of the old ball of fur.

You see, Roscoe was a tiny kitten when he had suddenly shown up at the station house one night after a stolen car bust. The thief had been brought into the station, booked and thrown into a jail cell until he could be transferred to the county prison the next morning. When the officers on duty had searched the stolen car for other items, Roscoe was discovered underneath the passenger seat, tiny, cold, scared and very hungry. He was immediately accepted into the station as the official resident "police cat". Everyone loved him and every officer made sure he was fed and warm during their shifts. Roscoe was part of the police station family and always would be. He was treated with the utmost respect and love.

Sarge jostled the thick fur around the old cat's neck and asked, "Ready for some lunch, big fella'? I'll go fill up your bowl and give you fresh water. You deserve that much, tough guy."

Sarge got up, pushed his chair back and headed into the meeting room where all of Roscoe's cat food was stored. Roscoe knew it would take him a few minutes to empty out his food bowl, rinse it out, dry it, and add more cat chow. He would also have to refill his water bowl and scoop out his litter box. Roscoe was looking at five or six minutes of opportunity to complete what he needed to do. He quickly set to work, pouncing his paws on Sarge's computer keys, pulling up search windows.

Quick, find the car license registration window, he thought.

Searching, searching, finally. Up popped the box to enter the numbers of the license plate. The tomcat quickly typed in FBH349 and in a matter of seconds, the information appeared on the screen, showing Roscoe to whom the car belonged and their address. He secured it to his memory: *589 E. Barnwood Drive.* His work here was done so he quickly hopped down off the desk, but made sure to leave the computer screen open to the search box with the license plate number and the address clearly showing on the screen. Sarge would definitely see this. And with that he and the two others were off down the hall, through the hole in the drywall, down into the basement and out the open window. They were headed in the direction of Barnwood Drive.

Sarge came back into his office and plopped his rather large bottom side down into his office chair. He looked up at the computer screen, stared in confusion, and rubbed his bristly head.

"Now how the heck did this come up?" he wondered out loud.

Chapter 15

The dogs were so tightly squeezed together that they could hardly breathe, but they couldn't take the chance of the two snoring men to hear them. Mermilo started giving directions.

"OK, listen gang. If we want to get out of here, we need to work together. Mookha and Thor, see that rope over there? When I quietly open the kennel door, I want you two to tip toe over to that work bench and grab it. Stand there until I give you further directions. Got it?" he asked.

"Got it, dude. I'm all over it. You can count on me," Mookha replied.

"Hey, I'll do anything to get us out of here," Thor quickly piped in.

Mermilo then motioned for Chico to step forward. "Chico, I need you to be our lookout. You have a keen eye and notice everything. When Mookha heads towards the workbench to retrieve the rope, you dart outside and keep a sharp eye on anything and everything. If you see or hear Henry, their boss coming then start barking like you've just spotted the biggest enchilada in your life. That will let us know that we need to hurry. Got it? Can you do that?"

"Holy guacamole, senior. I am good at that. I can bark loudly. My neighbors get very mad when my owner lets me out in the early morning because I am so loud. And I love enchiladas. Especially the kind with beef bits and lots of gravy and chunks of bone in them. Yes, senior, you can count on me. For sure senor, for sure."

Chico jumped up and down and twirled around on his two hind legs. Finally, he could help someone. It was the mission of a lifetime. His dream was coming true.

"Beauregard, I need you front and center," Mermilo commanded.

The old Bassett hound slowly hoisted his body up off the dusty ground and waddled over to the group. Looking up at Mermilo, he smiled, ears perked up, ready to hear his assignment in this kennel breakout operation.

"Here's your job. Because you are about the size of a large overstuffed footstool, you are going to be the obstacle the thugs fall over. As they stand up and head towards the kennel, you are going to be in the exact spot where they will trip over you. They are going to be in a daze from hastily being awakened and won't be expecting you to be there. You will take them by surprise. Think you can handle that? I'm counting on you old guy. How about it? Are you up for it?" Mermilo asked.

"You bet I am, Mermilo. I am always ready for a goooood time and this sounds fun. Thanks for thinking of meeeee," Bulregard answered.

He was so proud to be able to participate. He may be old and slow, but he was short, stocky and out of sight—the perfect footstool to trip over.

Mermilo walked over to Queenie, who stood there licking her shiny coat to make sure no tangles were forming in the dusty environment. He stopped in front of her and stared into her dazzling blue eyes.

"Well, Queenie," he inquired, "are you ready for the performance of your life?"

She batted her eyes with those long lashes, winked at him, and answered, "You bet. As long as my coat doesn't get messed. Nothing is worth that. But I am glad I can help somehow. Now, where should I stand where the lighting is the best to show off my exquisite beauty? You have noticed my beauty, haven't you?" She asked.

"I have, Queenie. You are very beautiful, indeed. Now, here's your job. You are going to do what you do best – stand there and look beautiful. Be a beautiful distraction."

He chuckled. Queenie was ecstatic. This was one performance she wouldn't have to practice. She was more than ready. Besides, she did this performance every day of her life.

With everyone understanding their parts and several verbal run-throughs of what was going to happen, the operation was ready to go down. Everyone held their breath as they prepared for the breakout of the century.

Chapter 16

Fats and Purina tore down the street as fast as their fuzzy little paws could carry them, with Roscoe in the lead. He knew the precise location of any address in town. After living in the police station for over eight years, he could tell you every major crossroad in the entire community, as well as zip codes, neighborhoods, and side streets. He knew exactly where he was headed.

They raced along through the center of town, cutting behind the grocery store parking lot and taking a shortcut through the alley between the hardware store and the drug store, finally exiting three streets over. They kept running, not stopping to take a breath or to speak. They had to get there quickly. As they turned the corner onto a dirt road, the street sign above them read 'E. Barnwood Drive'. They raced further down the gravel road until they came to a rundown wooden-planked farmhouse set back in the trees. Yep. This was it. There, sitting in the dusty driveway, was the old red four-door, with the license plate that read FBH349. All three felines slowed down to a halt.

They had to approach with caution. No one was in sight as far as they could see, but at any moment someone could come barreling out of the door of the old shelter in the side yard. They crept along slowly and quietly. As they passed the house, they could see a grubby, older gentleman standing at the kitchen sink. He looked like he was washing something; dishes maybe. They couldn't tell from their location. They continued on through the yard, like ninjas, unseen and unheard and ready to dive in while trying to avoid detection at all costs. They headed towards the shelter.

"Jump up onto the drainpipe and onto the rooftop and see if you spot anything, Fats," Roscoe ordered. "Do it quickly before anyone shows up here in the yard and discovers us."

Fats immediately pounced with all his might up onto the eaves spout and continued onto the roof.

"Nope. No one as far as the eye can see, Roscoe," Fats announced.

"OK then. So far so good," Roscoe replied. "Purina, conduct a perimeter walk and report back. Go." Roscoe commanded.

"Ay, ay Sir. Captain's orders being obeyed." Purina chimed with a huge cat grin.

He took off and started slinking around the entire outside of the shed, looking and listening for anything or anyone suspicious.

Roscoe knew how to take control of a hostage situation. He had been a police station cat for many years. He had seen it all; heard it all. Eavesdropping many times as calls came in on the station radio, he fully understood reports from officers about securing a crime scene, negotiating with kidnappers, pursuing getaway cars, and all that good stuff. He was well prepared to secure the area and take it back into the hands of the good guys.

Chapter 17

Meanwhile, inside the shed the dogs were preparing to initiate their escape. Everyone was in place, waiting for the cue that the show was ready to start. Mermilo quietly opened the gate. Thank goodness it didn't squeak. He gently tiptoed over to the two men snoring in the chairs. He checked each one to make sure they were in a deep slumber before motioning for the others to take their places. Both were so sound asleep that they didn't even flinch when there were gunshots flying from the movie playing on the television. The coast was clear. Mermilo nodded his head and motioned with his paws for everyone to get into place. The show was about to begin.

Chico quickly hustled over and quietly creaked open the front screen door of the shelter. His little body slipped outside, the whole time keeping his eyes peeled for any movement whatsoever. He was the lookout dog—a big job for a little pooch. He was going to show them that he could do it. His eyes darted left then right. His tail was wagging faster than a hummingbird's wings could flutter. His little tongue was hanging excitedly out of his turned up mouth.

"I must keep watch. I must keep watch. I must keep watch," he chanted in his head.

Vlad and Mermilo quietly positioned themselves alongside the workbench where the television stood. Mookha and Thor moved stealthily in front of the two men's chairs. Beauregard was ready to swiftly place his body underneath the thugs' feet when it was time. Everyone was holding their breath. If this didn't work, they would never get another chance. The thieves would either guard them nonstop, or make their move and get rid of them…however they were planning. It was now or never.

Mermilo glanced around the dimly lit room. *"Everyone ready?"* His eyes asked the question. As he glanced around at them, each slowly nodded, holding his/her breath. He did a final look at the scenario and gave the go ahead nod with his head.

Queenie started whimpering softly in a forlorn sort of way. When the men didn't stir, she whimpered a little bit louder. Roy shuffled a bit in his seat. Again, Queenie whimpered as if she was hurt. Roy sat up in his chair, rubbed his eyes and glanced at her. She started to limp. Roy became more alert and nudged Shep.

"Hey Shep, I think something's wrong with that fancy dog over there. It sounds like she's crying. And she's moving kind of funny."

Shep snorted in a low guttural manner and sat up slowly. He scratched his head and face, turned to look in

68

the kennel's direction, and his mouth suddenly dropped open. He jumped out of his chair like he had been sitting on hot coals and stood straight up staring in Queenie's direction.

"Holy cow, Roy. Where are all the other dogs? Where are they? Henry is going to wring our necks, not to mention cut us out of the money. Roy, you were supposed to be watching them. Where in blue blazes are they?"

Roy jumped up, swirled around and almost lost his balance. "I was supposed to be watching them? You were supposed to be watching them. What is there to watch when they're locked up in a kennel? Don't try to pin this one on me, Shep."

At that moment, Queenie straightened herself up, waltzed over to the kennel door, kicked it open and pranced out. She stood there looking at them with a snooty look on her beautiful silken face.

"Come and get this beautiful dog, boys. If you can, that is."

And with that she turned and trotted haughtily to the door leading outside the shelter. Roy and Shep scrambled over each other to get to the afghan hound as fast as they could. They were yelling and blaming each other at the same time, grabbing at the other's clothes to try and get to the dog first, making quite a ruckus.

Quietly, Beauregard stepped out and stood ever so still behind the thugs as they rambled and scrambled. Roy grabbed Shep, trying to wrestle him to the ground, blaming him for the escape. Shep lunged back, defending himself against Roy's false accusations. The two had a tight hold of each other, rumbling and bumbling around like two rambunctious teenagers.

In doing so, they failed to see the large Bassett hound position himself right behind the backs of their legs. They shuffled some more and as they stumbled backwards, fell right over Beauregard, flying to the floor in a ball of complete helplessness.

Mookha quickly moved in with the rope. He took one end in his mouth as Thor joined in, quickly grabbing the other end. Vlad, Max and Mermilo hastily joined in to help with the tie-up. The five dogs worked together wrapping the two men's hands and legs securely together so they couldn't move. Mermilo and the gang were going to see to it that these crooks would never kidnap another dog again.

Roy and Shep were in absolute shock as they watched the dogs tying them together like professional cattle ropers. Roy could barely make out the shapes of the dogs as the dust from the dirt floor had been stirred up in the turmoil.

Shep was stuttering "What the ???" while choking and coughing from all the dust that had been kicked into his wide gaping mouth.

The dogs worked fast and furiously. When the thugs were secured, Mermilo yelled for everyone to get out of the structure.

"Now." he screamed, as they all headed for the door.

They tore out of there like a pride of lions after their evening dinner on the Serengeti, not looking back once.

Chapter 18

Chico was keeping his watch, prancing one way, then the next, when all of a sudden out of the corner of his eye he spotted movement as Purina rounded the corner on his perimeter check. Without even investigating, the little taco of a dog started yipping at the top of his lungs.

"Ayayayay. Ayayayaya. Ayayayay."

Poor Purina stopped dead in his tracks and, of course did what came naturally to a cat…he puffed up like a sponge in a bucket of water.

"Phhhhhhhhhhhhhht." he hissed loudly.

From the end of the building, Roscoe yelled as loud as possible.

"On the roof now, Purina." he hissed in his authoritative police cat voice.

With one leap and bound, Purina was immediately up on the drain pipe and on top of the roof, joining Fats. Roscoe appeared from the other end of the roof.

"Boys, I don't know what's going on, but we'll just ride it out up here," Roscoe assured them. They watched from above as things below began to unfold.

All of a sudden, the door of the structure burst wide open, with dogs of all shapes and sizes flying out in every direction. There was barking at decibel levels one had never heard before. The excitement was astounding. Of course, this aroused old Henry in the kitchen of the house. He could hear all the hoopla and immediately knew something was wrong.

The back door of the house flung open with an ear shattering crash and Henry bound down the porch steps like a bolt of lightning from a storm cloud. He launched his body towards the swarm of canine hostages, trying his hardest to retain them. The three felines on the rooftop watched from above as the chaos below turned into mass hysteria. The dogs were escaping and there was nothing any of the thugs could do. As they watched Henry running around like a chicken with his head cut off, old Roscoe knew immediately what needed to be done.

"Follow me," he hollered at the other two cats.

He sprang towards the edge of the roof and without hesitating for even a split second, flung his furry body with legs, paws and claws outstretched onto the back of old Henry. Roscoe dug in with all his might and hung on for dear life.

Taking the clue, Fats hurled himself onto Henry's head, digging into the nearly bare scalp with his sharpened claws and attaching himself to the wrinkly skull like glue. Henry nearly had a heart attack grabbing at his head and trying to yank the cat off. Purina quickly followed the leads of the other two cats.

"Cannonball." Purina wailed out loudly as he plunged through midair onto Henry's chest. Claws once again dug into the leathery skin of the old codger, causing him to holler as loud as he could while grabbing at the cats, arms flailing through the air.

This act of hysterical commotion gave the dogs just enough time to make it out of the shelter, down the driveway and establish a good solid head start back towards town. As soon as they were out of sight, the cats all piled off onto the ground and took off like wild rabbits.

Just as they were tearing out of the driveway, police sirens were heard in the distance. Roscoe immediately detected they were getting closer. As the three cats rounded the bend in the road, four squad cars wheeled onto E. Barnwood Drive, heading straight for the wooden planked house.

Henry heard them coming and rushed inside the structure. He stopped dead in his tracks with a look of utter defeat on his face. There in a heap on the dirt floor was a huge mass of two tied up, dusty, sweaty chubby men, both clamoring at the same time, blaming each other for not watching the dogs. They were arguing so loudly Henry just shook his head and threw his hands up in surrender. He slowly turned back around towards the door, walked out into the bright sunlight, and patiently stood, waiting to greet the police. At this point he would do anything to get away from these two bumbling fools.

The police cars screeched to a dusty halt. Four officers bustled out of the cars with guns drawn. One approached Henry and placed heavy metal handcuffs on the old man's wrists. Four other officers hurried into the structure, only to be surprised by the hilarious sight that met their eyes.

This was definitely the sight of the canine abductions. The kennel inside the dimly lit sweltering shelter was the cops' first clue. Upon further searching, pictures of each dog were found, along with a map of their expected travel routes, a price list for each breed, and names of potential buyers for every one of them.

Roy and Shep had not even realized that the police were there. They were still continuing with their obnoxious arguing and throwing of accusations at each other. The police cut them loose, handcuffed them up, and brought them out of the structure to join Henry. All three men were arrested, read their rights, tossed into the backseat of the squad cars and hauled downtown for booking. The charge: *dognapping*.

Chapter 19

Mermilo and the rest of the hostages kept running as fast as their legs could carry them until they were downtown, standing in front of Clausen's Clipper Clinic. They all came to an abrupt stop, hearts beating heavily in their chests, wild gulps of air ventilating through their panting mouths. They had actually done it. They had escaped their imprisonment. They were free canines once again. And the bad guys had been caught. It took several minutes for the realization of the past day's events to hit them, and it hit them hard.

No one knew what to say to each other. As they stood there getting their wits and emotions in order, Mermilo cleared his throat and began to address the entire group. With a hint of sadness in his voice, Mermilo managed to speak.

"Wow, you guys…and girl. We did it. We actually did it. That was incredible. We couldn't have managed our escape without the efforts of every single one of us. We all played a major part in our victory. I can't thank you enough."

He turned to face the little Chihuahua, that was drawing attention to himself, because he couldn't keep his little rat sized body on the ground. He was jumping up and down with excitement and joy. Panting like a little hyena and grinning from ear to ear while doing flips and turns to celebrate his freedom and his new friends, he felt elated just knowing that he had actually helped someone today.

"Chico, way to keep an eye on things. I knew you were the right one for that job. Your sharp vision and distinct warning yelp gave us a heads up that we needed to act fast. And for that, you will always be my friend, near and dear to my heart," Mermilo announced.

"Ay, senor. It is I who is grateful that I could help you. Never again will I be ashamed if anyone mistakes me for a sewer rat. I am proud to look like a rat—we took care of three rats today. Did we not? Chico began to dance and sing right there in the middle of the sidewalk in front of Clausen's Clipper Clinic…

> *Ay ya ya ya*
> *I am the masked tan bandito*
> *I take care of crooks,*
> *Yes, I take care of them.*
> *I sound off the bark*
> *So that we all can scram.*

Thank you, Senior Mermilo, for trusting me."

He wagged his little tail, did another flip in the air, then gave Mermilo's cheek a quick lick with his tiny tongue to show his appreciation and love. Mermilo smiled and nodded. The little long-haired Chihuahua took off down the street and slipped into a side alley and disappeared out of sight. Mermilo turned back to the group and addressed the Afghan hound.

"Queenie, I must admit that you were absolutely magnificent in getting their full attention. You truly are a natural at being beautiful, and I must say…you are one of the most beautiful decoys any operation could ask for. I will always be indebted to you and your services."

"Oh, Mermilo. That is so kind and thoughtful of you to say that. However, in my defense, I was born to be beautiful and I am a natural. Don't you think? It is this voluptuous golden silky coat of mine. Do you now understand why I was so concerned about the dust matting it up? They wouldn't have given me a second glance if several of my long flowing hairs were out of place. However, I am truly pleased I could be of help. Mermilo, my beautiful heart thanks you. I really must be heading home now. It's time for my combing and I simply can't miss that. Tah-tah."

Mermilo just shook his head, smiling. He guessed even in the face of danger, true personality always shines through. Queenie proved that to everyone in the group.

As Queenie pranced away in only the way Queenie could prance, all the others were still congratulating each other.

"Mookha, I've never seen a dog move that fast in securing an enemy. I can now actually picture in my mind how you must handle your dogsled in the ice and snow. If it was anything like the lightning manner you handled that rope with those two crooks, it's no wonder you're always a winner. I know you'll do great at the Ididarod this year. I'll be watching for you on the news. Oh, and Mookha…Thanks. Thanks for being a huge help, but most importantly, thanks for being a friend," Mermilo said gently.

Mookha broke out into a huge broad Siberian Husky grin; the one where every tooth in his mouth was showing. He laughed and jokingly responded.

"Yeah, sure. It was fun. I mean, it was a great breakout. What an adventure. It was almost as exciting as the time we were up in the Yukon hauling the sled at too fast of a speed. We suddenly turned a sharp bend, and the weight of the sled caused the rope on one side of the rig to break. The entire sled and all its contents veered over the edge of the cliff. The team, along with my master, were dangling by the remainder of the rope that was left. I was the only one that still had solid footing so it was up to me to pull the sled, my master and the five other dogs to safety. All my workouts really paid off. My face was all over the papers. Yeah, like I said, it was *almost* as fun. Hey, hope to see you around sometime, Mermilo. Thanks for the memory of today."

Mookha turned and slowly started to head his way home. Mermilo sat quietly watching him leave.

"Wow," Mermilo thought. "That dude has an ego the size of Alaska. It's fitting for him though, I guess."

Mermilo turned to the Labrador.

"Thor, you were a huge help today. Don't take this the wrong way, but I'm glad you showed up. Your 'fetch' practices with your master have really paid off with swiftness and grace. Keep it up." Mermilo joked.

"It was an experience, I'll admit that. But I've had enough fun for one day and I need to be on my way home. My master is probably worried sick about me. Not to mention I'm really hungry." Thor announced.

He smiled at the group, turned around and sprinted down the street. He really did move quite gracefully for the big fellow he was.

Mermilo turned back to the rest of the dogs still standing in front of Clausen's.

"Beauregard, I owe you a huge thanks, my friend. You may be slow, but you are precise. You angled yourself in the perfect location to create havoc with those two huge brutes. Without your help, they would have nailed us all and we would still be sitting in that kennel. You were amazing."

"Aaaaaaah, shucks. It was nothing. I just did what comes naturally. I sit wherever my bottom plops doooooown. No thank you is needed. But a thank you goes to yoooou, Mermilo. It's nice to be free again. Now if you don't mind, I'm going to go hooome. It's dinner time followed by bedtime and I need my orthopedic pillow. That dirt floor bothered my backside. So long, Mermilo."

With that, the old dog started to slowly waddle down the sidewalk, whistling a soft tune to himself.

Still standing in Mermilo's presence was Max, the greyhound athlete of a dog. He seemed to be in rather a bit of a hurry to get on his way, yet he could not bear to leave without saying a proper goodbye to Mermilo.

"It was sincerely a pleasure meeting and working with you this afternoon. You certainly have a way of getting things accomplished. I am truly indebted to you, as now I will be able to attend my important evening event at the Children's Hospital. They, as well as I, will be forever thankful. Thank you and good luck with your important evening event, whatever it may be. Goodbye. Goodbye."

He turned toward home and took off in a sprint, more than likely to get dressed in his tuxedo and head to his special appearance.

"Good luck to you, too, Max," Mermilo called but Max was already too far away to hear him.

Mermilo turned around and Vlad was the only one left. They stood there chuckling with each other. What a group of canines. They had all truly felt thankful for each other and their talents in getting themselves out of that situation. Mermilo rested silently for a few moments. He stared at the ground, then ever so slowly looked up at Vlad. Vlad had been watching Mermilo the whole time.

"I am really thankful that you showed up ven you did. Vee needed another mastermind in planning a breakout. You vere our answer to a prayer. I thank you comrade for your friendship, your loyalty, and your trust. You vill always be a hero in my heart."

Vlad became very solemn and sounded deeply sincere, glancing only a few times at Mermilo, as he reflected upon his words. He was afraid that if he looked the retriever in the eye, tears would form in his eyes. Russian wolfhounds are not meant to be sentimental dogs. They are strong, stern, tough dogs bred for their bravery and courage, not their hearts of gold.

Mermilo knew Vlad was struggling to keep his emotions hidden, so he tried to make it as easy as possible for him.

"Vlad, it's OK. It is no big deal, so don't take it upon yourself to make it a big deal. We all wanted to get out of there and we all worked together, just as I said earlier. So let's just drop it, OK? Hey. I've got to get moving. I have a HUGE night ahead of me and I'm a dirty, filthy mess. I'm going to have to be on my way so I can get cleaned up as much as possible and hope for the best. Wish me luck, Vlad."

"Good luck, Mermilo. I hope whatever it is you are doing tonight turns out the way you want it, my friend."

Mermilo wagged his tail, nodding and smiling, and both dogs turned to go their own way. He had only trotted a few steps down the sidewalk when all of a sudden he stopped and turned.

"Hey Vlad," he yelled back to the hound.

Vlad turned to look.

"Thanks. Thanks for everything. I'll never forget you. You will always be a friend to me," Mermilo yelled.

Vlad smiled, turned back around and continued on his way home.

All of a sudden, like a streak of lightning, three furry fuzz balls came galloping down the sidewalk, racing out of control. Their hair was so mat0+ted with dirt and dust they looked like they had just been tossed out of a tornado. They veered and swerved just in time to scoot around each of the big canines as they continued on their way.

"Hey, you smelly mutts. Get out of the way. Why you think you can take up the whole sidewalk is beyond me." Roscoe screamed, as he sailed past at top speed.

"Yeah, don't you have some stupid pet tricks to be performing for a human somewhere?" hollered Fats, following on Roscoe's tail.

"Did anyone tell you beasts you are useless animals?" wailed Purina, bringing up the rear.

The three cats continued their sprint, heading for the police station. They wanted to get there so they could see some REAL action—three dognappers being thrown in the clink. It was going to be a great night.

Mermilo and Vlad followed the cats with their eyes, turned back to glance at each other and started chuckling to themselves. At the same time, they both turned and headed their separate ways. Before they had walked very far, four police cars went flying past, sirens blaring at top volume.

Vlad and Mermilo stopped once again, turned and looked at each other. This time they smiled and gave each other a knowing nod. They had done their part and justice had been served.

By the time the squad cars reached the police station, all of the dogs had dispersed and were no longer standing together on the sidewalk in front of Clausen's Clipper Clinic. Still howls and barking of celebration were heard simultaneously in various areas of town. The dogs had won. They all knew it and were rejoicing together in harmony.

Mermilo sprinted at a fast pace to his house, shot up through the front yard, around the back through the gate, and into the kitchen through his doggie door. He raced up the stairs and into the bathroom. He needed to get cleaned up for tonight.

He looked in the mirror and was astonished at how tired and ragged he looked. It was at that moment he realized how exhausted he really was.

"Oh Miss Purelove, please forgive me for not having a freshly trimmed coat. If you only knew what I have been through today." he thought to himself.

She would understand as soon as he explained it to her. He was positive in his mind. He would apologize when he picked her up, and as they dined on an appetizer of Rawhide Rockefeller, he would tell her the whole story. He knew she would be in awe of his quick thinking and bold actions. He just knew it. With that thought still in his mind, he realized that he had just enough time for a quick dog nap. Just a few minutes would give him spunk, personality, and most of all, the energy to stay alert and spontaneous.

He slowly padded into his room and plopped his body down on his big comfy overstuffed pillow and in no time at all, was snoring away in doggy slumber.

Chapter 20

All at once, something went off in Mermilo's mind. His head shot straight up as he tried to become alert. Where was he? Why was he on his pillow? He should be up, getting ready for his big night out on the town with the pooch of his dreams. Oh no. Did he oversleep? Had he missed his date? Would she think he had stood her up? This was too much for Mermilo to fathom. After all, it had taken him so long to work up the nerve to ask her out, let alone talk to her. Oh my, oh my, this couldn't be happening.

He jumped out of bed and rushed to the bathroom. He was frantically searching through cupboards and drawers to find a towel, a comb and his toothbrush. He didn't have time to stop and think about anything except getting ready for his big night. This was a disaster. How could this be happening?

He was capable of getting himself out of a hostage situation yet couldn't get himself up in time for a date? He was about to cry when he turned and there, sitting in the doorway eyeing him suspiciously, was a tan and white long-haired cat. The look on the feline's face was one of confusion.

"Hey Mermilo. What's up? Is something wrong? You look like you have just seen a ghost. Are you OK? It's not like you are naturally OK, but you seem less OK than normal. For a dog, I mean. Dogs are never OK, but you know what I'm getting at, right smelly?" Fats the cat spurted at Mermilo.

"Fats, I don't have time for your remarks right now. I'm late for a very important event. I was supposed to pick Miss Purelove up at seven, but by the time on the clock, it's already eight-thirty. I am so late. We will never get a table at any restaurant at this hour," Mermilo responded, choking back his disappointment.

"Man. And dogs are supposed to be so smart." Fats muttered, shaking his head in disgust. "Hey dog-breath, it's eight-thirty all right…in the morning; Tuesday morning. Hello? What did you eat for dinner last night? Liver? You know what liver does to your insides and your brain. You must have been dreaming."

Fats hunched his back, did a little "pfhhhhhhht, pfhhhhhht", and was off down the stairs to grab some grub from his food bowl by the kitchen table.

Mermilo stood there staring at the spot where the fluff ball had just been insulting him. Was Fats correct? Was it really just a dream? Or nightmare one might say? Really? Honestly, truthfully, really? Mermilo raced to the window just in time to see the sun coming up over the Wilson's house next door. "Oh dear golly goodness. It was a dream. But, wow, it felt so real." he thought to himself.

All his friends had been in it. Vlad, Beauregard, Max, everyone. Even that snooty Afghan Hound down the street, Queenie. How in the world did she make it into his dream? He didn't exactly care much for her. Oh, he was nice whenever they would cross paths. But he certainly didn't seek her out to strike up a conversation. No, sir.

Mermilo was beside himself with relief. Today was his salon appointment. He hadn't missed it at all. Oh what a glorious morning. His heart swelled with excitement at the thought of the evening that lay ahead of him with the adorable poodle.

He raced down the stairs and into the kitchen to say good morning to his master, Stan Dudley, whom he loved very dearly. He loved him even more dearly now, knowing that he hadn't been taken from him after all, and that everything was fine. He nibbled on his breakfast, savoring every wonderful bite.

Yes, today was going to be beautiful. After finishing his morning meal, he gathered his things, tidied up his pillow and left the house for his morning grooming appointment with his favorite salon stylist, Cheryl.

As he stepped out onto his front porch, the sun hit his soft fur, warming not only his outer coat but his inner heart as well. He pranced down the front steps and onto the sidewalk. He turned and headed towards his styling salon, Clausen's Clipper Clinic, humming a lively tune. He sauntered down his street and turned left onto Hazelnut Street, the way he always went when he had an appointment with Cheryl.

He trotted merrily along, not noticing the old red four door car parked on the other side of the street with two big brutes sitting in the front seat.

Yes, today was going to be a beautiful day. Nothing would be able to spoil it for him he thought, as he continued on his merry way toward Clausen's Clipper Clinic.

About the Author

Jenny Uzelac is a 4th grade teacher who loves every day with her students experiencing new adventures, insights, and writing opportunities. In her leisure time she enjoys running, cooking, and being with her family. Originally from Pennsylvania her family has lived in Arizona for 15 years..

Made in the USA
Middletown, DE
15 March 2022